彼得的聚會

Peter's Party

Mandy and Ness

Chinese translation by David Tsai

MILET

在彼得的聚會上，有許多美
味的食品可以品嘗。
彼得舔著一個
冷冰冰的 . . .

At Peter's party, there are
lots of tasty things to try.
Peter licks a
cold and icy . . .

彼得吮吸著一
個**又酸又香**的 . . .

Peter sucks a
sour and zesty . . .

彼得**嘎吱嘎吱**
地嚼著一些．．．

Peter munches
some **salty** . . .

彼得吃著他最喜歡吃的
食物。那是一塊加了**香料**的 . . .

Peter eats his favourite
food. It's a **spicy** . . .

彼得一口一口地咬
著一塊**甘甜**的 . . .

Peter bites a
sweet and sugary . . .

彼得喝著一杯
濃厚乳製的 . . .

Peter drinks a thick

and **creamy** . . .

啊呀！
打了個飽嗝！

Oooops!
Burp!

For George B. Turner
M.

Peter's Party / English–Chinese

Milet Publishing Limited
PO Box 9916, London W14 0GS, England
Email: orders@milet.com
Web site: www.milet.com

First English–Chinese dual language edition published by
Milet Publishing Limited in 2000
First English edition published in 1998 by Scholastic Ltd

ISBN 1 84059 147 1

Typeset by Typesetters Ltd, Hertford, England
Printed and bound in China